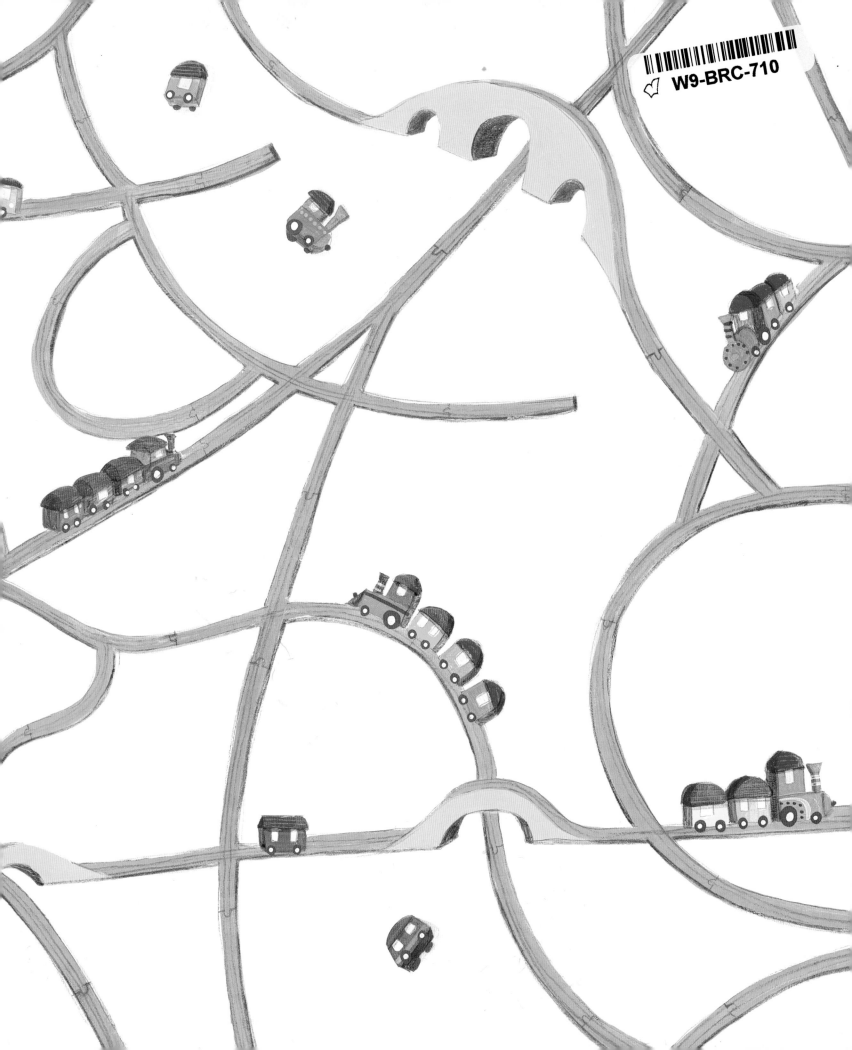

To my little blueberry - J.A.

tiger tales
5 River Road, Suite 128, Wilton, CT 06897
Published in the United States 2014
Originally published in Great Britain 2014
by Little Tiger Press
Text and illustrations copyright © 2014 Judi Abbot
ISBN 13: 978-1-58925-163-2
ISBN 10: 1-58925-163-6
Printed in China
LTP/1400/0892/0314

For more insight and activities,
visit us at www.tigertalesbooks.com

TRAIN!

by Judi Abbot

tiger tales

Little Elephant loved trains.

When
Mommy and Daddy said,
"Dinner!"

Little Elephant said,
"Train."

For a special treat, Little Elephant's Mommy and Daddy took him on a real train. He was VERY excited, until . . .

Cat didn't want to play trains.

Car!

Penguin didn't want to play trains either.

"TRAIN!"

stormed Little Elephant.
He had a terrible train tantrum.

"Train! Train! Train! Train!
Train! Train! . . ."

"TUNN

everyone shouted, jumpin

When the train came out of the tunnel, everyone was in a heap. And their toys were all mixed up . . . .

"Train?" said Cat.

"Plane?" said Little Elephant.

This was new. This was . . . FUN!

Train - plane - digger - digger! Train - plane - car!

Train - plane - car! Train - plane - car! Digger - digge

"You've learned a lot of new words today!"
said Little Elephant's Mommy and Daddy.

Little Elephant nodded.

He'd learned a lot of new words. And one very special one . . .

"Friends!"

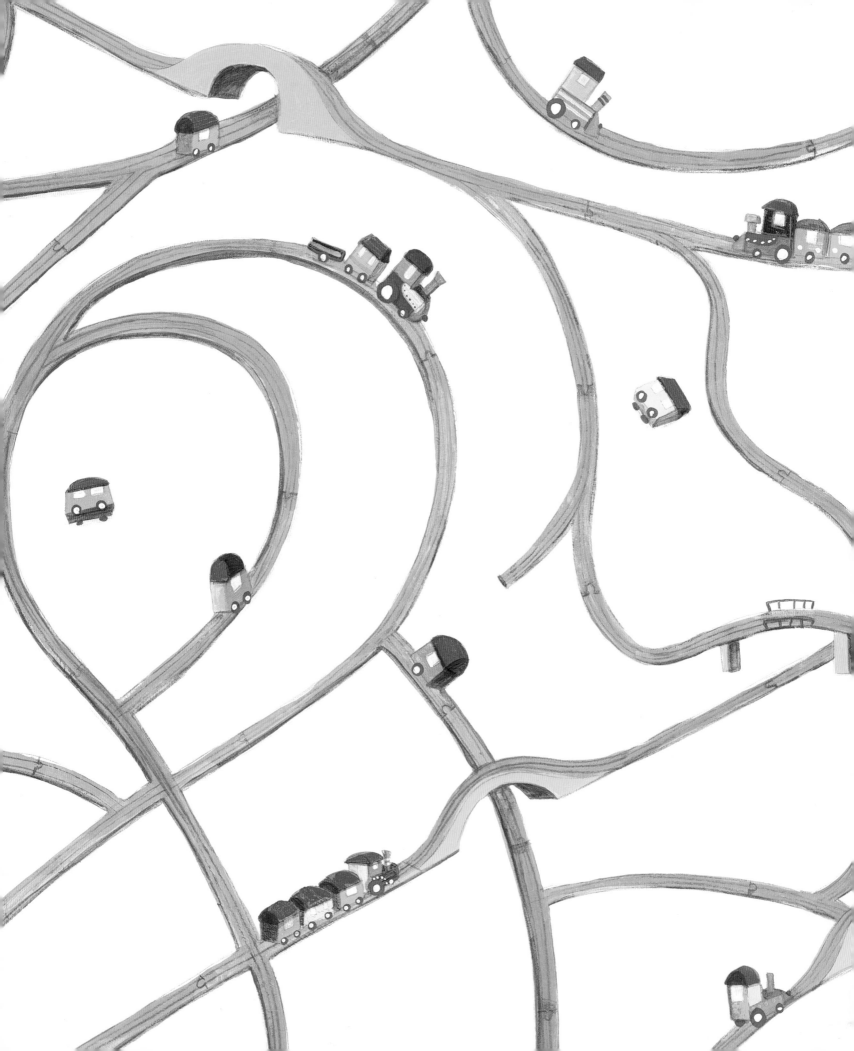